Little
Troll

First published in 2007 by
Franklin Watts
338 Euston Road
London
NW1 3BH

Franklin Watts Australia
Level 17/207 Kent Street
Sydney
NSW 2000

A CIP catalogue record for this book is available
from the British Library.

ISBN 978 0 7496 7150 1 (hbk)
ISBN 978 0 7496 7293 5 (pbk)

Series Editor: Jackie Hamley
Series Advisor: Dr Hilary Minns
Series Designer: Peter Scoulding

Printed in China

Franklin Watts is a division of
Hachette Children's Books.

Little
Troll

by Penny Dolan

Illustrated by Lisa Smith

FRANKLIN WATTS

LONDON•SYDNEY

Penny Dolan

"When I'm writing, I like to listen to the words in my head. So no noisy neighbours please, though goats might be okay."

Lisa Smith

"When I was a child, we had a goat, so I know how Troll feels! I hope that you will enjoy the pictures in this book as much as I enjoyed drawing them."

Little Troll lived under a bridge.

He played with
his little friends.

He swam happily
in the river ...

... until the Bully
Goats came –
Little Bully Goat,

8

Middle-sized
Bully Goat,

and Great Big
Bully Goat!

They stamped across
that bridge by day ...

... and by night.
Poor Little Troll!

15

One day, suddenly,
the bridge creaked.
Then it cracked.

CRASH! Into the river went those bad Bully Goats.

"Help! Help!" cried
the Bully Goats.

Little Troll saved them.

Little Troll and the Bully Goats lived *quietly* ever after!

Notes for adults

TADPOLES are structured to provide support for newly independent readers. The stories may also be used by adults for sharing with young children.

Starting to read alone can be daunting. **TADPOLES** help by providing visual support and repeating words and phrases. These books will both develop confidence and encourage reading and rereading for pleasure.

If you are reading this book with a child, here are a few suggestions:

1. Make reading fun! Choose a time to read when you and the child are relaxed and have time to share the story.

2. Talk about the story before you start reading. Look at the cover and the blurb. What might the story be about? Why might the child like it?

3. Encourage the child to reread the story, and to retell the story in their own words, using the illustrations to remind them what has happened.

4. Discuss the story and see if the child can relate it to their own experience, or perhaps compare it to another story they know.

5. Give praise! Remember that small mistakes need not always be corrected.

**If you enjoyed this book,
why not try another TADPOLES story?**

Sammy's Secret
978 0 7496 6890 7

Mop Top
978 0 7946 6895 2

Stroppy Poppy
978 0 7496 6893 8

Charlie and the Castle
978 0 7496 6896 9

I'm Taller Than You!
978 0 7496 6894 5

Over the Moon!
978 0 7496 6897 6

Leo's New Pet
978 0 7496 6891 4

My Sister is a Witch!
978 0 7496 6898 3